HEN LAKE

written and illustrated by

MARY JANE AUCH

Holiday House/New York

For Janeen Marquez, Beverly McDonnell, Laura Smith-Weyl, and
Joyce Farrell—fellow members of the world's only five-part quartet!

Copyright © 1995 by Mary Jane Auch
ALL RIGHTS RESERVED
Printed in the United States of America
Library of Congress Cataloging-in-Publication Data
Auch, Mary Jane.
Hen lake / written and illustrated by Mary Jane Auch. — 1st ed.
p.   cm.
Summary: Tired of the bragging of Percival the peacock, Poulette
convinces the other hens in the barnyard that they can outperform
the boastful bird in a ballet she creates.
ISBN 0-8234-1188-5
[1. Chickens—Fiction.   2. Peacocks—Fiction.   3. Ballet dancing—
Fiction.]   I. Title.
PZ7.A898He   1995   94-47218   CIP   AC
[E]—dc20
ISBN 0-8234-1270-9 (pbk.)

Poulette was an unusual hen. She didn't enjoy doing the same things as the other hens in the barnyard. She didn't scratch for bugs or take dust baths. She never even tried to lay an egg.

Poulette could think of nothing but her dream to become a ballerina. So she spent almost every hour of every day dancing.

One day, Poulette was practicing her pirouettes when her friend Philomena flapped over. "Follow me!" she said. "You have to see the strange new bird the farmer just brought home with him."

"A new hen?" squawked Poulette. "Is he replacing one of us?"

"No, it's not a hen. It's a . . . I don't know what it is."

All the hens rushed into the barnyard.

"You're right," whispered Poulette. "It's definitely not a hen."

"Look at that scrawny neck," said Zelda. "Maybe it's a goose."

The bird turned suddenly. "I'm neither hen nor goose. My name is Percival and I . . ." There was a rustle of feathers, and right before their eyes, Percival did an amazing thing.

" . . . I am a peacock, the most *glorious* bird in the universe!"

"Wow!" clucked Gertrude. "Get a load of those tail feathers."

Percival strutted around the barnyard, so all the hens, ducks, geese, and pigeons could admire him.

Poulette cleared her throat. "Welcome to our farm, Percival. I hope you'll be happy here."

"I doubt it," said Percival. "It's rather ordinary, compared to my last home." With that, he spread his wings and flew up to perch in a nearby tree.

Poulette watched him for a moment, then went back to her practicing.

"What on earth are you doing?" asked Percival.

"Dancing. If someone asks me to star in a ballet, I want to be ready."

Percival laughed. "You call *that* dancing? I'm much more graceful than you are. I could star in a ballet if I wanted to."

"If you're so wonderful, come down here and show me," Poulette said.

"I don't feel like it," said Percival. "Maybe later," and he flew off.

That afternoon, some pigeons were singing for Poulette.

"I just love your music," Poulette said to them.

"You call that music?" squawked Percival. "Those pigeons are just making noise, but I have a magnificent voice."

"If you're so terrific, let's hear you sing!" demanded Poulette.

"I'm not in the mood," said Percival. "Maybe another time."

The next day, Poulette was dancing in the garden while the other hens were busy scratching for bugs.

Percival swooped down and perched on the scarecrow. "If I wanted to scratch for bugs—which, of course, I don't—I could catch more bugs than all of you put together."

"Oh, for heaven's sake," said Poulette. "Is there anything you *don't* do better than everyone else?"

"Of course," said Percival. "I'm not good at being ordinary like you hens."

"That does it!" said Poulette. "I'm sick and tired of listening to you brag. I challenge you to a talent contest on the night of the next full moon. Would you rather sing or dance?"

"Or catch bugs?" offered Philomena.

"I'll sing and dance at the same time," said Percival. "I don't do bugs."

Philomena sighed. "Percival was right. We hens are ordinary, except for you, Poulette."

"You are *not* ordinary," said Poulette. "You could all be dancers." She looked at her friends. "Why didn't I think of this before? I don't have to wait for someone to make me a star. I'll create a new ballet for the contest, and you'll all be in it. I've always wanted to dance with a corps de ballet."

"Nonsense." Claudine snapped up a beetle. "We have work to do."

"Besides," added Gertrude. "We don't know how to dance."

"I'll teach you," said Poulette. "We'll call the ballet . . . *Hen Lake!* You can be the Hen Maidens, and I'll be the Hen Queen."

The hens protested, but Poulette finally convinced them to start lessons that very afternoon.

As the days went by, Poulette was a patient teacher.
"One more time . . . and one and two and . . . Oops!
Watch where you're going, Philomena! That's good,
Gertrude, now try to point your toes."

Percival's laughter interrupted them. "Dancing
chickens," he screeched. "What a hoot!"

"Just ignore him," said Poulette.

"We were perfectly happy being ordinary hens," squawked Claudine. "Now you have us making fools of ourselves."

"Keep practicing," said Poulette. "You're getting better every day."

And Poulette was right. Although the hens still couldn't manage leaps and spins, they were doing their very best.

"We need music," said Poulette, so she called in the pigeons.

"We can't sing," they protested. "Percival said we make noise, not music."

"Don't pay any attention to that pompous peacock," said Poulette. "Your singing sounds wonderful to me."

After that, the birds sang for every rehearsal, but it didn't help much.
When Gertrude zigged, Zelda zagged, and they were getting cranky.
"My feet hurt," grumbled Gertrude.
"Oh, go lay an egg," squawked Zelda.
"Lay one for me," said Philomena. "I'm pooped!"

"We need costumes," Poulette announced one day. She cut tutus from some curtains she found in the trash. All the hens helped, but Poulette stitched alone into the night using glittery fish scales for sequins. She barely finished in time. "You're lovely," she said, as the hens tried on their tutus.

"Really?" asked Zelda. "I don't feel lovely."

On the night of the full moon, there was a buzz of excitement as the audience gathered. Percival was the first to perform. He strutted slowly across the stage, stopping to pose every few feet, while singing an aria from an opera.

"He's not really dancing," whispered Poulette. "He's just showing off."

"We can do better than that," said Zelda.

But then Percival started turning—slowly at first—gradually spinning faster and faster. For his finale, Percival leapt through the air while hitting a high note. He landed on one foot and fanned his glorious tail. The audience rose to its feet. "Bravo!" shouted a goose. "Percival will be the winner. He's magnificent!"

Poulette was helping the Hen Maidens with their last minute makeup touches when Percival came offstage. "Interesting costumes," he said, smirking. "Do I smell fish?"

Claudine yanked at her tutu. "We can't leap and spin like Percival. We're going to look like idiots."

"If you believe in yourselves, you can do anything," said Poulette.

She signaled for the pigeons to begin the overture. "That's your cue," she said, pushing the Hen Maidens onto the stage. "Break a drumstick!" The Hen Maidens bourréed into the moonlit barnyard. They were halfway through their first number when a dark cloud slid over the face of the moon.

Lightning split the darkness. Poulette saw her dream of *Hen Lake* crashing with the thunder that rumbled overhead. When she thought things couldn't get any worse, the sky opened up and they were pelted with hail. "Run for cover!" she shouted.

Just then, a gust of wind lifted the Hen Maidens into a series of grand jetés. Gertrude even had her toes pointed! A small whirlwind caught Zelda and set her spinning like a top. She did sixteen fouettés without missing a beat.

As suddenly as the storm had begun, the black cloud let go of the moon and moved on. The pigeons started the music for the Hen Queen's solo, and Poulette stepped onto the glittering stage. As she danced, she felt her heart would burst with joy.

When she finished, the audience roared. Poulette called the Hen Maidens to take a bow.

"They're cheering for you, Poulette," said Zelda. "We weren't really dancing. The storm just blew us around."

"Remember how it felt?" said Poulette. "You can do it again. Try it!"

Zelda attempted a wobbly turn. "It's no use. I'm a klutz."

"Use your imagination," said Poulette. "Feel the wind rushing through your wing feathers. Believe in yourself!"

Zelda closed her eyes, took a deep breath and did thirty-two fouettés. "I did it!" she squawked. "I really did it!" Soon all the hens were spinning and leaping. The audience went wild.

When the crowd shouted "Encore!" Percival started sneaking away.

"Look! Percival is leaving," said Claudine. "He got what he deserved. He sure looks pathetic."

"I'll perk up his feathers," said Poulette. "We can afford to be kind." She turned to the audience. "For our last number, Percival will join us."

The peacock brightened immediately and rushed on stage. "Just follow my lead," he said. "I'll make you hens look good."

"We already look good, Percival," said Zelda. "You follow *our* lead."

During the final curtain call, Philomena whispered, "Percival isn't any more special than we are, is he?"

"Of course not," said Poulette. "An ordinary hen can be anything she wants to be, but under all those fancy feathers, a peacock is just a long-necked chicken."